# The Screaming Mean Machine

ISBN 0-590-48013-8

12 11 10 9 8 7 6 5 4 3 2 1          4 5 6 7 8 9/9

Printed in Hong Kong

First Scholastic printing, May 1994

# The *Screaming* Mean Machine

The Screaming Mean Machine

Joy Cowley

David Cox

Scholastic Inc.

New York   Toronto   London   Auckland   Sydney

Last summer at the amusement park
I went on a ferris wheel ride
in a seat that stopped at the top
then swung like crazy
and dropped down the other side.

I wasn't scared.

I went on the ghost train in the dark
through a tunnel of howls and groans
and the rattle of skeleton's bones
and I wasn't scared of that either.

Last summer I went on a lot of things —
the parachute drop, the octopus swings,
the mountain slide, the water ride,
and the rocking Viking boat.

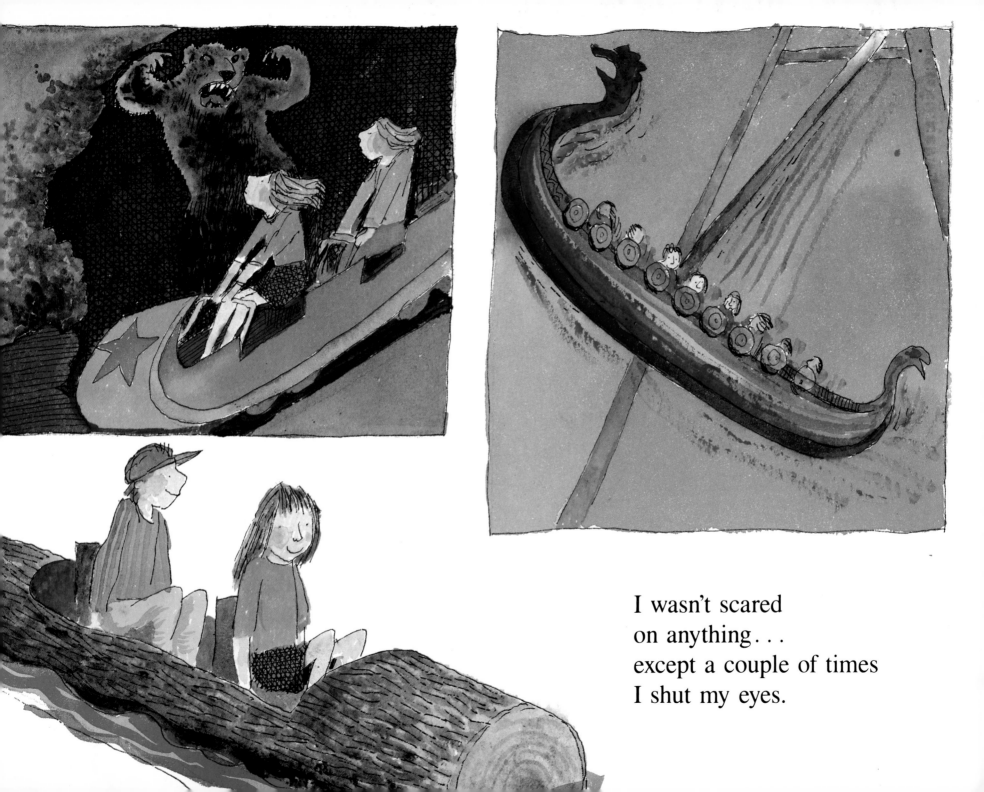

I wasn't scared
on anything...
except a couple of times
I shut my eyes.

But all of last summer I was too small
for the biggest and fastest ride —
the roller coaster that everyone calls
the Screaming Mean Machine.

The rest of the family went on it —
my Mom, my brother Rick, my cousins,
my Dad who sat in the car
with his hands in the air
and said he was going to be sick
(although he kept going back for more) —

YOUR
HEAD
MUST
REACH
MY HAT
TO RIDE

while I had to stay down on the ground and watch them all.

But this year I've grown
like a string bean
and now I'm not too small.
I'm big enough and strong enough
and brave enough and tall enough
for the Screaming Mean Machine...

except, perhaps, just maybe,
when I think about it,

I could wait another
month or more
to be positively,
absolutely sure.

"Sit with me
in the front seat,"
my brother Ricky says.

We're in the car
and a bar comes down.
The bar is sticky with cotton candy.
And I think I'm too young,
after all.
Next year is a better idea.
Next summer would be dandy.
I think I've changed my mind
and now I wonder
how I get out of here.

I say to Rick,
"What happens if the wheels
come off the track?"

He says, "They can't."

"But suppose they did?"

"They'd just put them back,"
he says.
Then he looks at me real close
and says,
"Hey, don't you freak on me!"

"Who's going to freak?"
I want to know.

"You're scared!" he says.
"I can see!"

"You can't see anything!" I laugh.
"Ricky, you're out of your tree!"

The car jerks.
There is a long rattling sound
like chains in a dungeon.
We are being pulled up
high off the ground,
high up the Screaming Mean Machine,
so high up a mountain of track
that all I can see is sky.

Then I lean over and look back
a long way down at Mom and Dad
who are like little dots
of confetti on the ground.

The car stops at the top
and my stomach flips.
But I'm not going to freak.
I'm not!

Then the car
begins to move.
Oh-oh!

So fast I can't breathe.
Race, race, straight down.
Wind in hair.
Wind in face.
My brother yelling, "Yay-eeee!"
I hold onto the bar.

Faster. Faster.
Can't feel.
Can't see.
Blur of speed.
Noise of wheels.

People screaming,
everyone screaming...
except me.

And faster! Oh!
I wish I'd never come!
Oh, someone, please!
Please, someone,
make it stop!

Down to the bottom and up again
with a clatter and shudder and bump.
My hair is flapping in my face.
Water is running out of my eyes.
There's a lump in my throat.
I can't make a sound.

The car swings around and up, up
over again.

My brother yells
but I can't hear the words.
I'm holding onto the bar,
so hard that the bone
in my hands is like stone.

We are coming to the loop on the ride,
a circle like a gigantic hoop.

Up the side,
then upside down.
The park comes up over my head
with the ferris wheel like a rising sun.
I see the water ride, the carousel,
then — *wooosh!*
We're down the other side.

Ricky has his hands in the air.

"You'll fall out!" I shout.

But he doesn't hear.
He doesn't care.

We're at the corkscrew bit
where we sit
pushed hard back in our seats
while the car goes around and around,
twisting fast,
everything rushing past,
like a river in a flood,
tracks mixed up with sky
and sky mixed up with ground.

Ricky brings his hands down
and grabs the bar, like me.
He looks as though he might
be a little bit frightened, too.

Now we're rushing into darkness,
with our car leaning sideways
in a spiral of flickering lights.
Red, blue, silver, green.
I see blobs of color moving
over Rick's hands and face.
Green, silver, blue, red.
Like stars in space, and meteors.
But I can't see where we are.

The car tips further over
and the people behind us yell.
They think they're going to fall
down the wall of the Mean Machine,
but I know very well it's another trick
to scare us and make us scream.

Then, with a turn and a twist
we break out into the sun
and there's the station ahead
and Ricky is saying,
"Hey! Wasn't that fun?"

And I'm saying to him,
"Some kid's got sticky stuff on this bar.
Look! It's all over my hands."

And I'm saying to him,
"Who said I was going to freak?
Who said I was looking scared?"
as the cars rattle and creak to a stop.

I run down the steps
to meet Mom and Dad.
"That was the most fun
I ever had in my whole life!
I'm going to do it again..."

When?

"Right now!
This minute!
I can't wait to get back on it.
I'm going on another ride
on the Screaming Mean Machine."